OUR MOMS

OUR MOMS

Q. Futrell

Illustrations by CLARISSA FERGUSON

NEW YORK

NASHVILLE • MELBOURNE • VANCOUVER

OUR MOMS

Published in New York, New York, by Morgan James Publishing. Morgan James is a trademark of Morgan James, LLC. www.MorganJamesPublishing.com

The Morgan James Speakers Group can bring authors to your live event. For more information or to book an event visit The Morgan James Speakers Group at www.TheMorganJamesSpeakersGroup.com.

ISBN 978-1-68350-437-5 paperback
ISBN 978-1-68350-438-2 eBook
Library of Congress Control Number: 2017901577

Cover Design by:
Rachel Lopez
www.r2cdesign.com

Interior Design by:
Bonnie Bushman
The Whole Caboodle Graphic Design

In an effort to support local communities, raise awareness and funds, Morgan James Publishing donates a percentage of all book sales for the life of each book to Habitat for Humanity Peninsula and Greater Williamsburg.

Get involved today! Visit www.MorganJamesBuilds.com.

DEDICATION

I dedicate this book to every parent who is incarcerated and desires a relationship with their child. Do not lose hope! Your child loves you. Your child needs you.

I also dedicate it to every educator who is uncertain about how to deal with the uncomfortable topic of incarceration.

And to every child who deals with parental incarceration... YOU ARE NOT ALONE!

ACKNOWLEDGMENTS

I appreciate my husband for all his love and support. Without his prayers this would not be possible.

To my children, Alton, Arielle and Ajala: I love you all!

To my mom, who did her best to be a great mother in spite of her being incarcerated: Thank you!

To my family and close friends: Thank you for believing in me!

Hi, my name is Michael.

I love to ride my bike after school.

My favorite part about school is lunch.

Hello, my name is Anne.

I love to draw brightly colored pictures.

When I grow up I'm going to be an artist.

¡Hola, me llamo Jennifer!

I love solving hard math problems.

Yesterday my teacher asked the class a really tough question, and I was the only one who knew the right answer.

Hi, my name is Paul.
I love playing video games.
I am the best player in my town.
No one can top my high score!

"My mom did not follow the rules when she was home," said Paul. "Mine did not either," both Michael and Jennifer said.

Anne sat up and said, "My mom did follow the rules. She just hung around people who did not follow them, and she got in just as much trouble as they did. Now she is in prison too."

"I remember being so sad when my mom left," explained Anne.

"I did not understand what I did to make her leave," added Paul. "Did I play too many video games that upset her?"

"I kind of felt like it was my fault too," said Jennifer.

"Well, I wanted to know who was going to cook the tacos on Taco Tuesday since my mom would not be there." Michael shrugged and looked confused.

"I thought it was cool when my grandma sat down with me the night after the police left my house to tell me what happened," said Michael. "She told me my mom had made a choice that led to a consequence.

"Grandma explained that a consequence is what happens after you do something wrong. Like if you do not eat all your vegetables at dinner your consequence would be no ice cream for dessert! Boy, I hate that consequence," added Michael.

"I love my mom. I miss her every day," said Jennifer.

She smiled and said, "Each time we talk Mom tells me, '*Te Amo,*' to remind me that she loves me."

"I miss my mom too," chimed in Anne. "During our visits she always tells me to make sure I pick the right friends. Anyone who thinks it is cool to break the rules and not listen to the teacher is not my real friend," she said.

"I send my mom a new letter every week," Michael said proudly. "When Grandma and I visit we have to get up very early. I have to wear certain clothes, or they will not let me visit.

"Because it is so far, it takes forever to get there. I love going to visit my mom the most because of the candy I get from the vending machines while I'm there!"

"I love telling my mom about all the new levels I am on with my games," said Paul. "It is like she is keeping score for me because she reminds me of what I told her our last visit."

Paul added, "My mom assures me when she calls that I did not do anything wrong. She says she did not leave because of me but because of a bad choice she made. That makes me feel better." Paul smiled.

"We might look different and speak differently, but one thing we have in common is all our moms are in prison.

This does not mean we will go to prison," said Michael.

"It also does not mean we want to tell everyone where our moms are," added Anne.

"Having a parent incarcerated does not mean I am weird," said Paul.

"It simply means our moms made a wrong choice or hung out with the wrong friends; but they still love us. They just do not live with us right now," Jennifer said.

"It is good to know we are not the only kids who have moms in prison," agreed Jennifer, Michael, Paul and Anne.

ABOUT THE AUTHOR

Quniana Futrell, known as "Q. Futrell", is a woman of resilience and healing whose primary goal in life is to change generational stories. A trainer, author, speaker and talk radio host, she works with key groups critical to rebuilding families affected by incarceration. This mission was born from personal experience. Author Q was once broken, navigating a childhood with both parents incarcerated. Now a wife and mom, she also loves to help other moms, who look well put together but are broken on the inside, change their story! She is a New Jersey native and now resides in Virginia. When she is not advocating for families, she is spending quality time with her three supportive children and creating multiple business empires with her husband, Alton. She is a strong advocate for children in their early years. She believes in what Rita Pierson says, "Every child deserves a champion—an adult who will never give up on them, who understands the power of connection and insists that they become the best they can possibly be."

"Change the family...change the world!" —*Author Q. Futrell*

Let's Stay Connected:

@AuthorQ

Visit www.qunianafutrell.com for more information.

3P SUPPORT FAMILY INITIATIVE

Parents, Professionals, and Providers—take a deep breath. Guess what? Parental incarceration may **affect** families, but it doesn't have to **infect** them. I have developed a cure for this infection to help <u>rebuild</u> and <u>strengthen</u> families affected by incarceration:

3P Family Support Initiative

Our mission is to transform the lives of families affected by incarceration while promoting healthy home and school lives for the children.

PROGRAMS

Nurturing Beyond Bars™

Designed to assist parents, providers, teachers, and professionals with the necessary tools to create a healthy home and school environment for children affected by parental incarceration.

Parenting Behind Bars (PBB)™

Designed to help parents who are incarcerated continue to be or become "good" parents! PBB is an instructional program for correctional institutions to help decrease the recidivism (relapsing into crime) rate.

Teaching Beyond Bars™

This 1 to 2-hour professional development course provides a blueprint on how to confidently teach children who have a parent incarcerated. This training is designed for social workers, foster parents, and any other professionals who interact with children and families affected by incarceration. Additionally, our staff is available for speaking engagements geared towards inspiring your staff and audience to continue to make a difference in the lives of our future generations.

NOTE: All programs are structured to meet **your** institution's individualized goals and requirements.

Remember, it not only takes a village, but it also takes the proper tools and resources to raise a child.

To purchase our program for your school or organization, contact us today:

Email: info@ecefirm.com

Phone: (757) 598-2117

To download your **FREE** resource guide, please visit our website www.3Psupport.com

www.TheMorganJamesSpeakersGroup.com

We connect Morgan James published authors with live and online events and audiences whom will benefit from their expertise.

Morgan James
Speakers Group

Morgan James makes all of our titles available
through the Library for All Charity Organization.

www.LibraryForAll.org

2 1982 02943 9613   NOV - - 2018

CPSIA information can be obtained
at www.ICGtesting.com
Printed in the USA
BVOW05s2352271217
503860BV00005B/22/P

9 781683 504375